Words to Know Before You Read

valley

van

vents

very

video

view

violent

visit

Viv

volcano

www.rourkeeducationalmedia.com

Edited by Precious McKenzie
Illustrated by Louise Anglicas
Art Direction and Page Layout by Tara Raymo
Cover Design by Renee Brady

Library of Congress PCN Data

Volcano! / J. Jean Robertson
ISBN 978-1-62169-244-7 (hard cover) (alk. paper)
ISBN 978-1-62169-202-7 (soft cover)
Library of Congress Control Number: 2012952740

Rourke Educational Media
Printed in the United States of America,
North Mankato, Minnesota

rourkeeducationalmedia.com
customerservice@rourkeeducationalmedia.com • PO Box 643328 Vero Beach, Florida 32964

VOLCANO!

Counselor Quinn

Ollie

Zoe

Rodney

Viv

Written By J. Jean Robertson
Illustrated By Louise Anglicas

"Hop in the van. We are going to visit a volcano," calls Counselor Quinn.

4

CAMP
ADVENTURE

URE

5

"Look," says Viv. "There's a mountain with smoke coming out."

"That is a volcano. Steam or smoke often comes out of holes called vents," says Counselor Quinn.

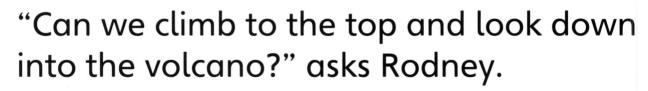

"Can we climb to the top and look down into the volcano?" asks Rodney.

Counselor Quinn answers, "We need to stay down in the valley. You can look through the binoculars for a good view."

"We are walking on something which is very strange, hard, and black," says Ollie.

"It is lava from the volcano," says Counselor Quinn.

Zoe asks, "What is that orange color sliding down the volcano?"

"Hot lava," says Counselor Quinn. "Let's go!"

"Look! The van brought us to the helicopter pad. Can we fly over the volcano?" asks Rodney.

"When we're over the volcano it looks violent," says Rodney.

"I can't wait to see Viv's video," says Zoe.

After Reading Word Study
Picture Glossary

Directions: Look at each picture and read the definition. Then write a list of all of the words you know that start with the same sound as *volcano*. Can you find any words in this book that have the *Vv* sound in the middle?

valley (VAL-ee): A valley is the low part of the land between two mountains.

van (VAN): A van is a vehicle that is bigger than a car and smaller than a bus. Vans can carry people or things.

vents (VENTZ): Vents are openings that steam or smoke can come out of.

 **video** (VID-ee-oh): A video is a recording that you can watch like a movie.

 **view** (VYOO): When you view something, you look at it.

 **visit** (VIZ-it): When you visit some place, you go to see it.

 **volcano** (vahl-KAY-noh): A volcano is a mountain with openings that lava, ash, steam, and smoke come out of.

About the Author

J. Jean Robertson, also known as Bushka to her grandchildren and many other kids, lives in San Antonio, Florida with her husband. She is retired after many years of teaching. She enjoys traveling, and has visited some volcanoes.

Ask The Author!
www.rem4students.com

About the Illustrator

Louise Anglicas is a Manchester born illustrator now living in the Staffordshire Potteries with her partner and two young daughters. Her first job was as a ceramic designer which involved reading Harry Potter books, and then designing mugs and children's breakfast sets based on them! Louise loves to travel with her family. Her favorite thing to do on holiday is go to waterparks with very big slides!